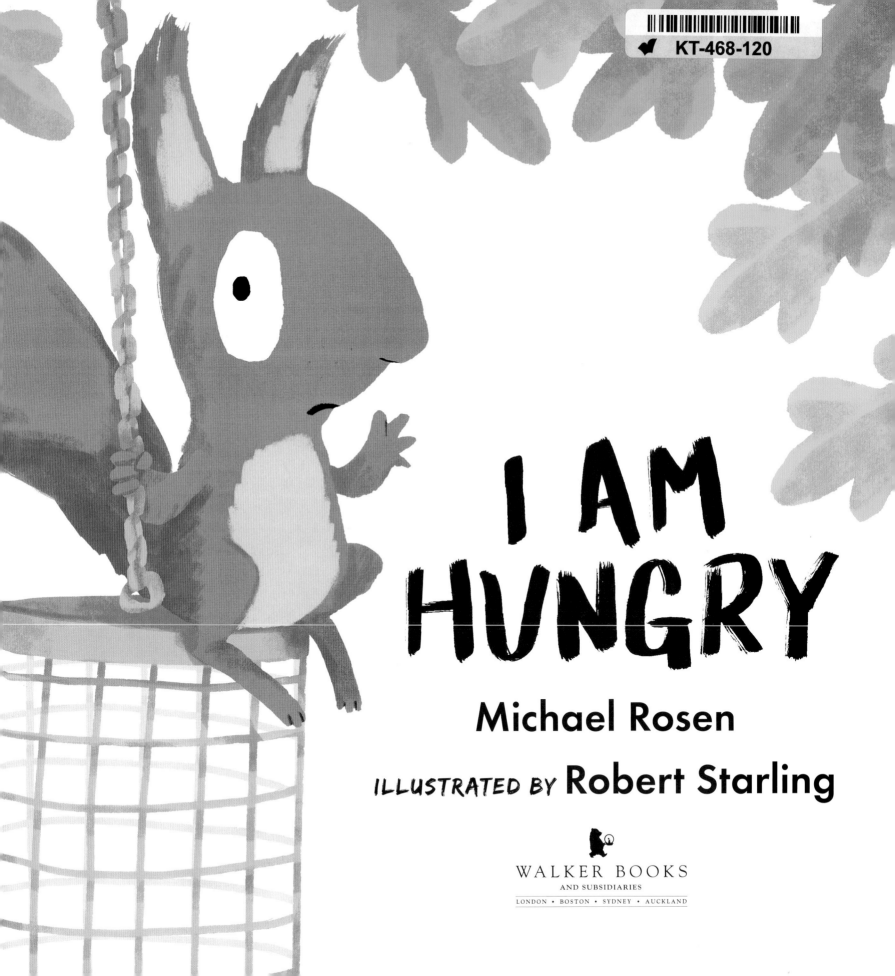

I AM HUNGRY

Michael Rosen

ILLUSTRATED BY **Robert Starling**

WALKER BOOKS
AND SUBSIDIARIES
LONDON • BOSTON • SYDNEY • AUCKLAND

I am
hungry.

REALLY
hungry.

I'm SO hungry, I'll ...

eat a bread roll,

popcorn in a bowl,

one plate of boiled rice,
two chocolate mice,

three slices of cheese,
a HUNDRED peas,

some fried fish,

a birthday wish,

a birthday cake:

a tummy ache.

A funny joke,

an egg yolk,

vanilla ice cream,

a very bad dream,

a gingerbread man,

Catch me, catch me, if you can!

a frying pan,

a nasty fright,

a dark and stormy night.

A signpost, a piece of toast,

a giant prune, a bit of the moon.

One last pea,

then I'll eat ...

me!

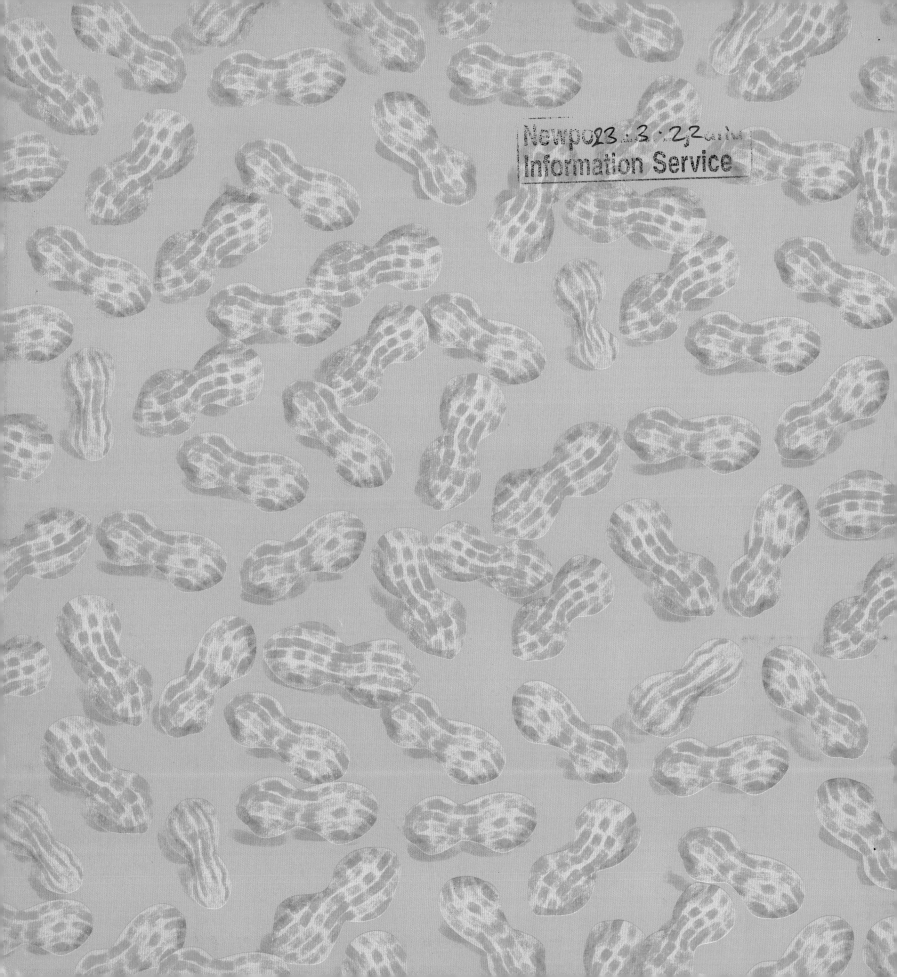

W.F.

A Note to Grown-ups

When I feel hungry I daydream about all the things
I could eat. Sometimes they are real things like cake
or a banana. Sometimes it's crazy things you
can't eat, like a dream or a wish. You could play this
like a game: take it in turns to think of real things
you'd like to eat and then mix them up with amazing and
impossible things. See who can come up with the craziest stuff!

For Joni from Zeyde Mick. M.R.

For Elsie. R.S.

First published 2022 by Walker Books Ltd, 87 Vauxhall Walk, London SE11 5HJ

2 4 6 8 10 9 7 5 3 1

Text © 2022 Michael Rosen • Illustrations © 2022 Robert Starling

The right of Michael Rosen and Robert Starling to be identified as author and illustrator respectively of this work has
been asserted by them in accordance with the Copyright, Designs and Patents Act 1988

This work has been typeset in Futura

Printed in China

British Library Cataloguing in Publication Data: a catalogue record for this book is available from the British Library

ISBN 978-1-4063-9666-9

www.walker.co.uk